Story and Illustrations by

Sean Sanczel

sanczel.com

Dedicated to Florida's hardworking dairy farm families and the millions
of consumers who enjoy healthy dairy foods.

© 2013 Florida Dairy Farmers

ISBN# 978-0-9888744-0-4
Library of Congress Catalog Number: 2013932491

THIS BOOK BELONGS TO:

Walkes-Watts Family child Care Home.

This is SunnyBell, a little calf who lives on a dairy farm in Florida.

She loves the farm because the farmers take such good care of all the cows.

When the cows want some shade, they rest in their stalls where fans and mist keep them cool.

And each cow has a comfy bed made of soft Florida sand.

Some even sleep on water beds!

They eat nutritious food that's specially made for cows.
Yep, it sure is great being a Florida dairy cow!

Every day, SunnyBell watched all the older cows line up to be milked.
But she didn't understand why they did this, so she decided to ask her good
friend, Maxine.

Maxine explained, "Two or three times a day cows produce nutritious and delicious, wholesome milk."

"Most cows can produce up to 7 gallons of milk each day!"

SunnyBell was filled with excitement. She always wanted an important job on the farm, and she knew this was it.

"I want to produce milk, too!" she yelled.

"Well, you can't produce milk just yet. You're still a calf," said Maxine.

"Once you're a little older and have a calf of your own, then you can make milk too!

That's the most important job here on the dairy farm."

SunnyBell knew there had to be an important job on the farm for her, so she decided to take a long ...

... long walk.

After a while,
SunnyBell looked
around and realized
she was lost!

She had somehow
walked right into town!

Across the street, there was a young boy running on the school track. He looked very tired.

He ran and tried to jump over a hurdle ...

... but fell flat on his face.

SunnyBell ran over to help the boy up.

"What's your name?" asked SunnyBell.

"Clyde."

"Well, Clyde, it looks like you could use a glass of milk!" giggled SunnyBell.

Clyde got back up to his feet. "No way! Milk is for little kids."

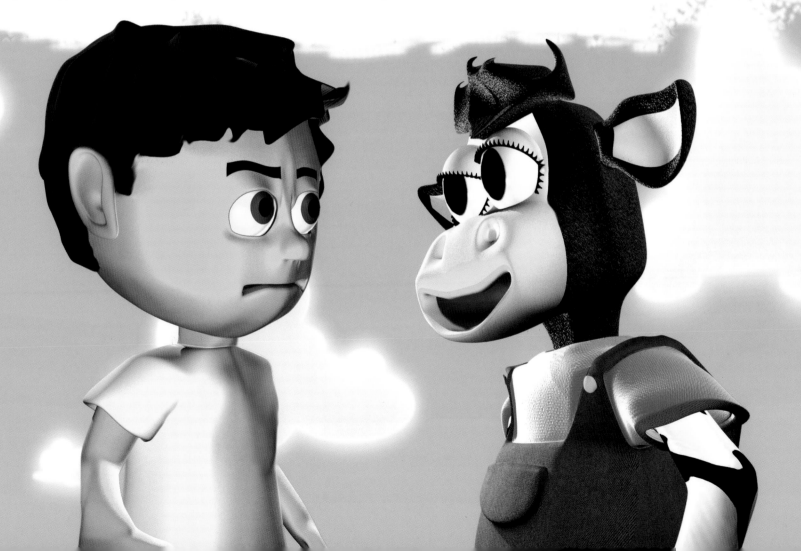

SunnyBell thought this was a very strange thing to say. She knew that milk was good for *everybody* - kids and adults!

She told Clyde that milk gives you strong bones and teeth and has 9 essential nutrients in every glass.

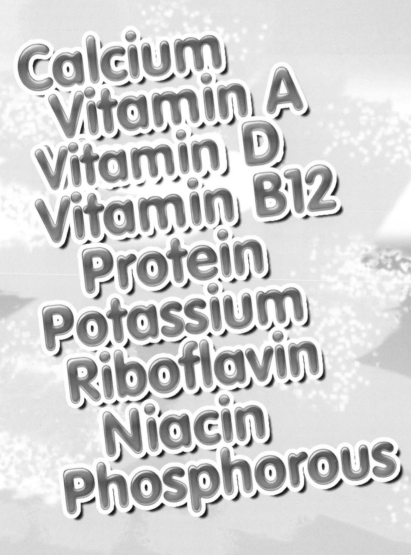

Calcium
Vitamin A
Vitamin D
Vitamin B12
Protein
Potassium
Riboflavin
Niacin
Phosphorous

"Really? That's awesome!" said Clyde. "Hey, wait a minute! Aren't you a cow?"

"Well, actually - I'm a calf," replied SunnyBell.

"Then what are you doing here in town?"

SunnyBell explained to Clyde how she got lost. "And now I don't know how to get home!"

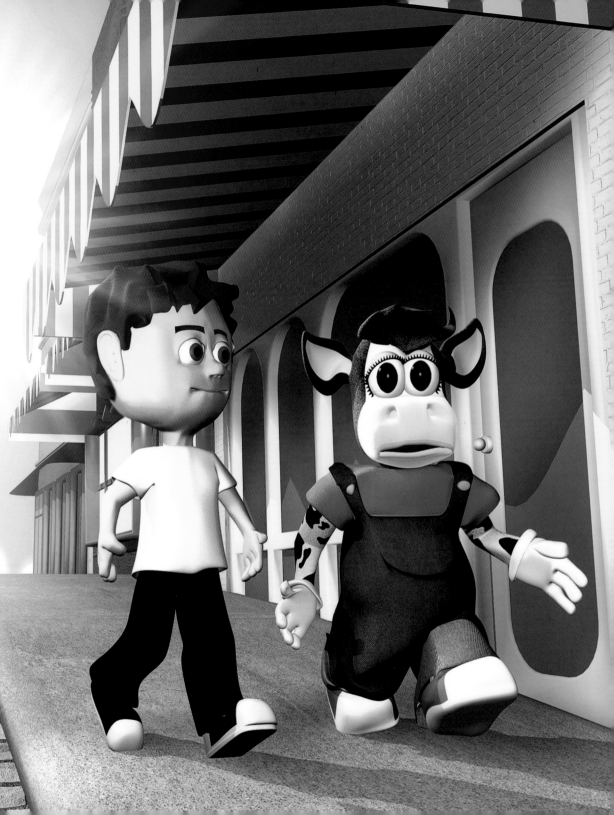

Clyde had an idea. "I know how to get you home! You come from the same place milk does, right?

Then we should go to the grocery store! That's where my mom gets our milk!"

Grocery Stor

The two walked down the aisles of the grocery store.

"Hmm, I don't see any cows here," said SunnyBell.

"Excuse me, did you say you were looking for cows?" asked a voice.

Clyde and SunnyBell looked up and saw that a bottle of milk was talking to them.

"We don't make milk here. Milk is delivered every day fresh from the dairy," explained Mr. Milk.

SunnyBell asked how she could find her way back to the dairy farm.

"Well," said Mr. Milk, "here in Florida we have more than 130 family-owned dairies."

"More than 130 dairies?" cried SunnyBell. "But which one am I from?"

Mr. Milk explained that they should go to the closest dairy farm, since milk has to be delivered fresh. There was one right down the road.

Clyde and SunnyBell thanked Mr. Milk and ran out of the store toward the farm.

Soon, the two made it back, and SunnyBell was reunited with Maxine.

SunnyBell thanked Clyde for being a good friend and helping her find her way home.

Then, she handed Clyde a fresh glass of milk.

Drink this. It will give you the energy you need to get back home."
Clyde chugged it down and said, "Mmmm ... I do like milk!"

Now try jumping that fence over there," said SunnyBell.

Clyde took off and jumped over the fence.

"That was easy! Thanks, SunnyBell! See you later!" yelled Clyde as he ran home.

"SunnyBell, I've got it!" said Maxine.

"Until you're old enough to produce milk here on the farm, you can teach kids about why milk is so good for them!"

And so, after SunnyBell's journey from the farm ...

... to the grocery store ...

... and back again, she discovered what she does best.

"Teaching people about nutritious and delicious milk is my job!" she said proudly.

So if you want to learn about milk, talk to SunnyBell - the happiest little calf on the Florida dairy farm.

For more activities, games and videos, visit floridamilk.com/sunnybell.